THE LITTLE GREEN MAN

By Mischa Damjan/Pictures by Maurice Kenelski
English version by Alvin Tresselt

Parents' Magazine Press/New York

This book was translated from *Das Gruene Maennchen 737*
© 1971 by Nord-Süd Verlag, Mönchaltorf, Switzerland

Library of Congress Catalog Card Number: 76-166286
ISBN: Trade 0-8193-0535-9, Library 0-8193-0536-7

Little Green Man Number 737 was sitting in his big comfortable chair and thinking. Presently he felt hungry. Reaching over to the control panel he pressed a button. In a moment a plate appeared with five green pills on it. Number 737 gulped them down and instantly felt full.

"How easy life is—" he thought, "and how boring." He pushed another button and the chair rolled over to the window. Below him he could see straight streets stretching into the distance. Hundreds of green people were going in all directions, but they were all standing still. Only the streets moved, carrying the people here and there.

He looked over the roofs of the green houses and he could see green saucers landing and taking off to fly in the green sky.

Number 737 yawned and pressed another button. The chair glided over to a second window. Here he could see green children in a green playground. They were playing with a robot cat and mouse. By moving levers he made the cat chase the mouse, but the mouse got away.

"How dull," said Number 737. "If only the mouse would chase the cat for a change, but the machine won't permit it. If only we had some real animals on this planet. Even a sparrow to fly across the sky. I must find some excitement somewhere."

He went up to the roof of his house and climbed into his flying saucer. At once it rose straight up and off into space.

With incredible speed he flew far away from his planet, past galaxies and suns until suddenly, right below him lay what looked like a rug of unbelievably beautiful colors.

"I must land and see what this is," he exclaimed, and carefully he brought the saucer down in a large field.

He had no sooner climbed out of his ship when a strange creature approached him. It had red hair and blue eyes and pink skin, and it was wearing a plaid skirt. "Hello," said the creature. "I'm MacTavish. Welcome to Scotland!"

"But you move and you don't have any antenna," exclaimed Number 737. "And those creatures over there," he said, pointing to a cow and two chickens. "They move, too!"

MacTavish laughed. "The big one is Fanny, my cow, and the other two are Reggie, my rooster, and Mary, my best hen." Then taking a good look at the green man he said, "And who are you and where did you come from?"

"I'm Number 737. I come from the green planet which is two galaxies beyond the Milky Way," he replied.

"Well, well," said MacTavish. "You must be hungry and tired after such a long journey. Come over to the house for a bite to eat."

While Number 737 rested in an easy chair MacTavish prepared some eggs and biscuits and a pot of tea for his strange guest.

"What beautiful pills these are," said Number 737. "Ours are always green. What are they made of? What button did you have to press?"

MacTavish laughed again. "Those aren't pills, they're eggs. And I didn't make them, Mary did, and she didn't have to press any buttons. Come, I'll show you how to eat them."

Never had 737 tasted anything so delicious. When he had finished, he relaxed with a sigh. He thought about the names of his new friends. MacTavish…Fanny…Reggie…Mary…

"I'd like to have a nice name, too," he said softly. "Mine is so ordinary. Everybody just has numbers where I come from."

MacTavish scratched his head and thought for a minute. "I have it," he said. "We'll call you Zym because that's the sound your saucer made when it came down."

"Zym…Zym," repeated the little green man. "Yes, that's a pretty name. Thank you."

It soon grew dark, and MacTavish showed Zym to his room. There was a large, comfortable bed with a soft down quilt. Zym snuggled in and he was soon sound asleep. His two antenna glowed red in his sleep because he was so happy. The barnyard animals gathered around outside his window, marvelling at this very strange creature who had come to visit Mr. MacTavish.

Early the next morning as the sun rose, Reggie crowed to wake everyone. Then after a hearty breakfast Zym went out to the barn to watch MacTavish do his chores.

He was amazed to see MacTavish milking the cow, but he was even more amazed to discover the fresh egg Mary had just laid in her nest. "What kind of animals do you have on your planet?" MacTavish asked him.

"Oh, we don't have room for animals anymore," Zym replied. "We need all the space for factories and houses and moving roads. We do have some mechanical cats and mice, but they are really only for playing with. You move different levers and the cat will chase the mouse. I find it very boring."

"How sad not to have any animals," said MacTavish. "But come, let's look around a bit."

As they crossed the meadow Zym suddenly stopped. "What is that? It looks like a small sun on the end of a green stick," he cried.

"It's a sunflower," said MacTavish, "and it's called that not only because it looks like the sun but because it likes to follow the sun as it crosses the sky."

"How marvelous," said Zym with delight. "Do you mind if I spend the day just watching this wonderful flower?"

So while MacTavish went off to plow in his fields, Zym passed the time watching the sunflower turn to look at the sun.

When MacTavish returned later in the afternoon he looked very tired.
"Poor man," said Zym. "Why do you have to work so hard?"

"It's the rocks in my field," said his friend. "Every year it gets harder
and harder to plow around them."

"Ha! Now I can repay you for your kindness," said Zym. He went
quickly to his saucer and came back carrying a strange machine.
"This is a disintegrating ray," he explained. "I'll soon make short
work of those pesky rocks."

He turned it on, and each time the ray hit a rock it dissolved into
fine sand.

"How can I ever thank you!" cried MacTavish. "What can I give you to
repay you for this favor?"

"There is only one thing I want to take home with me," said Zym,
"and that's the beautiful sunflower."

That evening as they rested after dinner, MacTavish began asking
questions about Zym's planet. "Instead of me telling you about it,"
said Zym, "why don't you come for a visit? I would like Mary to
come, too, so that my friends can see how she makes her pills."

Off they all went together, and Zym was sure to take along his sunflower.

In no time at all they were coming in for a landing. Zym radioed that he was bringing a very special guest, so by the time they landed there was quite a crowd to greet them. MacTavish had never seen so much green in all his life. And the people of the green planet had never seen anything as colorful as MacTavish, with his red hair, blue eyes, pink skin and plaid kilt.

Zym told them about his adventures on earth and how kind his friend had been to him. "Now I must show you a most wonderful thing," he said.

While everyone gathered around, a box was brought, filled with green straw. Mary settled herself in comfortably. In a short time she hopped up and began cackling, "Look-look-look what *I* did! Look-look-look what *I* did!"

Zym held up a beautiful white egg for all to see.

Leaving the crowd to marvel at this, Zym and MacTavish went to the roof of his house. In a large pot filled with green dirt they carefully planted the sunflower. It looked very lovely in the middle of all that green.

That night MacTavish prepared the egg for Zym while he, in turn, gave MacTavish a meal of green pills. MacTavish found the taste of the pills rather strange, but he had to admit that they filled him up.

Meantime, the animals back home were getting very nervous. They had seen MacTavish zip out of sight in the flying saucer, and they worried about whether they would ever see him again. All night long they anxiously watched the sky. But there was no need to be upset. Early next morning, just as it got light, there was the saucer back in the pasture, with MacTavish climbing out.

"I must return at once," said Zym. "But I will come to see you again. I promise."

MacTavish threw his arms around his new friend. "Yes, yes," he replied. I will have more sunflowers for you, and I will give you a chicken for your very own."

Then with a sharp *zym* sound the saucer rose up and disappeared into space.

Printed in the Netherlands by Meijer Wormerveer N.V.